# ICE TEAM

Based on the episode "The New Pup" by Ursula Ziegler-Sullivan
Illustrated by MJ Illustrations

A Random House PICTUREBACK® Book

Random House New York

© 2015 Spin Master PAW Productions Inc. All rights reserved. Published in the United States by Random House Children's Books, a division of Penguin Random House LLC, 1745 Broadway, New York, NY 10019, and in Canada by Random House of Canada, a division of Penguin Random House Ltd., Toronto. Pictureback, Random House, and the Random House colophon are registered trademarks of Penguin Random House LLC. PAW Patrol and all related titles, logos, and characters are trademarks of Spin Master Ltd. Nickelodeon and all related titles and logos are trademarks of Viacom International Inc.
randomhousekids.com
ISBN 978-0-553-52281-5
MANUFACTURED IN CHINA
10 9 8 7 6 5 4 3 2

Glitter effect and production: Red Bird Publishing Ltd., U.K.

One sunny day, the PAW Patrol was getting ready for a trip to see their friend Jake at the ice fields.

Suddenly, there was a loud roar, and a big truck rolled up.

"Presenting the PAW Patroller!" Ryder announced. "It's a Lookout on wheels. It can take us anywhere!"

A door opened in the side and a mechanical dog hopped out.

"Robo Dog will be our driver!"

As Ryder was showing the pups around the
PAW Patroller, Jake called.

"Hey, Jake! How are the ice fields?" Ryder asked.

"Amazing!" Jake declared. "Take a look!"
The screen showed snowy hills and an icy river.

Just then, Jake slipped on the ice, and the pups could hear him yell, "My phone! My maps! All my stuff!" Jake's equipment had splashed into the icy river!

"Jake's in big trouble!" Rubble exclaimed.
"Pups, get your vehicles," Ryder said.
The PAW Patroller's back door opened and a ramp came out. The pups quickly drove their vehicles aboard. Robo Dog started the engine and the PAW Patroller rolled into action.

At the ice fields, Jake was trying to get his backpack out of the water. But the riverbank was so icy that he began to slide in! Luckily, a husky pup pulled him out.

"Sweet save!" Jake said, then introduced himself.

"My name's Everest!" the pup exclaimed. "I rescued someone! I've always wanted to do a real rescue."

"We should probably get going," Everest said. "A storm's rolling in. I wouldn't want to lose my first real rescue in a blizzard. We can wait it out in my igloo. To get there, we can do this. . . ."

Everest flopped onto her belly and slid down
the hill.

"Belly-bogganing!" Jake shouted, taking off
after her. "Look out below!"

The two new friends slid along on the ice,
zooming past some penguins.

When the PAW Patroller reached the ice fields, the snow was falling hard. The team started to look for Jake. They quickly found his frozen phone and pack.

"This means Jake doesn't have any supplies," Ryder said. Then he noticed something in the snow. "Are those tracks?"

Chase gave the tracks a sniff. "That's Jake, all right! And he's got another pup with him."

"Those tracks should lead us to Jake," Ryder announced. "Let's follow them."

As Chase followed the tracks on the ground,
Skye took to the frosty air. "This pup's got to fly!"

Everest and Jake came to a narrow bridge that stretched across a deep, dark ravine. "My igloo is just across that ice bridge," Everest said.

"Will it hold us?" Jake asked.

"I hope so," the husky replied. "It's the only way to get over."

As they walked across, they heard a terrible cracking noise. The ice bridge was breaking!

Just as the bridge collapsed, Skye swooped in, catching Jake and Everest with a rope. But before she had carried them to the other side of the ravine, the rope broke.

"Jump!" Jake yelled.

Everest landed on a ledge, but Jake missed it.
He caught the edge with his fingers and dangled
over the dark ravine.

"Don't worry!" Everest yelled. "I've got you!"
She snagged Jake's sleeve and pulled him to safety.
"Yes—two rescues in one day!"

Everyone went to Jake's cabin on the mountain for roasted marshmallows—and a surprise.

"Everest," Jake said, "I could use a smart pup like you to help out on the mountain."

"And for saving Jake and showing great rescue skills," Ryder added, "I'd like to make you an official member of the PAW Patrol!"

"This is the best day ever!" Everest exclaimed, and all the pups cheered.